The Boxcar Children My

The Boxcar Children
Surprise Island
The Yellow House Mystery
Mystery Ranch
Mike's Mystery
Blue Bay Mystery
The Woodshed Mystery
The Lighthouse Mystery
Mountain Top Mystery
Schoolhouse Mystery
Caboose Mystery
Houseboat Mystery
Snowbound Mystery
Tree House Mystery
Bicycle Mystery
Mystery in the Sand
Mystery Behind the Wall
Bus Station Mystery
Benny Uncovers a Mystery
The Haunted Cabin Mystery
The Deserted Library Mystery
The Animal Shelter Mystery
The Old Motel Mystery
The Mystery of the Hidden Painting
The Amusement Park Mystery
The Mystery of the Mixed-Up Zoo
The Camp-Out Mystery
The Mystery Girl
The Mystery Cruise
The Disappearing Friend Mystery
The Mystery of the Singing Ghost
Mystery in the Snow
The Pizza Mystery
The Mystery Horse
The Mystery at the Dog Show
The Castle Mystery
The Mystery of the Lost Village
The Mystery on the Ice
The Mystery of the Purple Pool
The Ghost Ship Mystery
The Mystery in Washington, DC
The Canoe Trip Mystery
The Mystery of the Hidden Beach
The Mystery of the Missing Cat
The Mystery at Snowflake Inn
The Mystery on Stage
The Dinosaur Mystery
The Mystery of the Stolen Music
The Mystery at the Ball Park
The Chocolate Sundae Mystery
The Mystery of the Hot Air Balloon
The Mystery Bookstore
The Pilgrim Village Mystery
The Mystery of the Stolen Boxcar
The Mystery in the Cave
The Mystery on the Train
The Mystery at the Fair
The Mystery of the Lost Mine
The Guide Dog Mystery
The Hurricane Mystery
The Pet Shop Mystery
The Mystery of the Secret Message
The Firehouse Mystery
The Mystery in San Francisco
The Niagara Falls Mystery
The Mystery at the Alamo
The Outer Space Mystery
The Soccer Mystery
The Mystery in the Old Attic
The Growling Bear Mystery
The Mystery of the Lake Monster
The Mystery at Peacock Hall
The Windy City Mystery
The Black Pearl Mystery
The Cereal Box Mystery
The Panther Mystery
The Mystery of the Queen's Jewels
The Stolen Sword Mystery
The Basketball Mystery

The Movie Star Mystery
The Mystery of the Pirate's Map
The Ghost Town Mystery
The Mystery of the Black Raven
The Mystery in the Mall
The Mystery in New York
The Gymnastics Mystery
The Poison Frog Mystery
The Mystery of the Empty Safe
The Home Run Mystery
The Great Bicycle Race Mystery
The Mystery of the Wild Ponies
The Mystery in the Computer Game
The Mystery at the Crooked House
The Hockey Mystery
The Mystery of the Midnight Dog
The Mystery of the Screech Owl
The Summer Camp Mystery
The Copycat Mystery
The Haunted Clock Tower Mystery
The Mystery of the Tiger's Eye
The Disappearing Staircase Mystery
The Mystery on Blizzard Mountain
The Mystery of the Spider's Clue
The Candy Factory Mystery
The Mystery of the Mummy's Curse
The Mystery of the Star Ruby
The Stuffed Bear Mystery
The Mystery of Alligator Swamp
The Mystery at Skeleton Point
The Tattletale Mystery
The Comic Book Mystery
The Great Shark Mystery
The Ice Cream Mystery
The Midnight Mystery
The Mystery in the Fortune Cookie
The Black Widow Spider Mystery
The Radio Mystery
The Mystery of the Runaway Ghost
The Finders Keepers Mystery
The Mystery of the Haunted Boxcar
The Clue in the Corn Maze
The Ghost of the Chattering Bones
The Sword of the Silver Knight
The Game Store Mystery
The Mystery of the Orphan Train
The Vanishing Passenger
The Giant Yo-Yo Mystery
The Creature in Ogopogo Lake
The Rock 'n' Roll Mystery
The Secret of the Mask
The Seattle Puzzle
The Ghost in the First Row
The Box That Watch Found
A Horse Named Dragon
The Great Detective Race
The Ghost at the Drive-In Movie
The Mystery of The Traveling Tomatoes
The Spy Game

THE DOG-GONE MYSTERY

created by

GERTRUDE CHANDLER WARNER

Illustrated by Robert Papp

ALBERT WHITMAN & Company
Morton Grove, Illinois

Library of Congress Cataloging-in-Publication Data

Warner, Gertrude Chandler, 1890-1979.
The dog-gone mystery / created by Gertrude Chandler Warner ;
illustrations by Robert Papp.
p. cm. — (The Boxcar children mysteries)
Summary: When they take their dog, Watch, for obedience training,
the Alden children discover that some of the dogs in the class have vanished
and decide to try to solve the mystery of their disappearance.
ISBN 978-0-8075-1658-4 (hardcover) — ISBN 978-0-8075-1657-7 (pbk.)
[1. Mystery and detective stories. 2. Dogs—Training—Fiction.
3. Brothers and sisters—Fiction.] I. Papp, Robert, ill. II. Title.

PZ7.W244Do 2009
[Fic]—dc22
2008056048

Published in 2009 by Albert Whitman & Company,
6340 Oakton Street, Morton Grove, Illinois 60053.

10 9 8 7 6 5 4 3 2 1

Cover art by Robert Papp.

For information about Albert Whitman & Company,
visit our web site at www.albertwhitman.com.

Contents

THE DOG-GONE MYSTERY

CHAPTER 1

Watch Goes to School

"Look!" said Benny. "There's somebody we don't know at our mailbox." Benny was six years old and loved mysteries, even little ones.

Watch, the Alden children's dog, barked loudly. Then he raced down the lawn to the mailbox.

"Watch! Come back here!" shouted twelve-year-old Jessie. But even though Watch listened to Jessie best of all, he didn't listen now.

"It's a woman," said Violet, who was ten years old and the shyest of the four children. "She's wearing a purple shirt and she's putting something into our mailbox." Violet loved all shades of purple.

"Let's hurry," said Henry. "She might be afraid of Watch, even though he's just being friendly." At fourteen, Henry was the oldest. He felt responsible for his younger brothers and sisters.

The Aldens hurried down the long path that led to their mailbox, but when they finally got there, they were very surprised. Instead of barking and racing around in circles, Watch was sitting.

"Good dog," said the young woman at the mailbox. She had very bright red hair. "Up," she said, and Watch stood, his tongue hanging out. "Good dog," she said again.

"Wow!" said Benny. "Watch is doing whatever you tell him to do."

"Does he do what you ask him to do?" the young woman asked.

"Sometimes," said Jessie, "and sometimes

not. I'm Jessie Alden," she said. Then she introduced Henry, Violet, and Benny.

"I'm happy to meet you," said the young woman. "I'm Roxanne Sager. Just call me Roxanne."

"What were you doing at our mailbox?" asked Benny. "You aren't a mailman."

"No," laughed Roxanne, "I'm not." Then she gave each of the Aldens a bright yellow flyer.

Benny could read the headline, which said *Dog Gone Good*.

"It's about a new dog training school," said Violet as she read.

"Right here in Greenfield?" Henry asked.

"That's right," said Roxanne. "I've decided to start my own business, a dog training school. I named it Dog Gone Good, because I want to help everybody have a dog-gone-good dog."

"You must love dogs," said Jessie.

"I do," said Roxanne. "And dogs seem to like me—don't you, Watch?"

Watch barked happily and wagged his tail.

"Maybe you'll decide to bring Watch to dog training class," said Roxanne. "The first one starts this afternoon." She looked at the children. "All four of you can come with Watch. That way you can all learn how to ask your dog to behave. And now," she said, "I have a lot more flyers to give out." Roxanne waved goodbye to the Aldens and walked down the road to another mailbox.

The children watched her go.

"I love Roxanne's hair," said Benny. "It's so red!"

"And her shirt is so purple!" said Violet.

Jessie asked, "Did you see how Watch did everything Roxanne asked him to do?" Jessie looked down at their dog, who looked back up at her.

Henry opened the mailbox and took out the mail. The Aldens walked back up the path to the big house where they lived with their grandfather. After their parents had died, Henry, Jessie, Violet, and Benny had run away because they didn't want to stay with their grandfather. They had never met him and thought he was mean. So they hid in the woods and lived in an old boxcar. They found Watch in the woods, too. But their grandfather found them, and it turned out he wasn't mean at all. He brought them to his house to live. He even had the old boxcar moved to his backyard. The children used it as a clubhouse.

"What do you think?" Henry asked. "Should we take Watch to training class?"

"I don't know," said Jessie. "He listens to us most of the time."

Violet was still reading the yellow flyer. "This says that you can help your dog be safe by training it," she said. "It says a well-trained dog won't run out into traffic."

"Or jump on people," said Henry as he read over Violet's shoulder.

Benny was kneeling down, playing with Watch. "If we take Watch to dog school," said Benny, "*we'll* get training, too."

"Yes," laughed Henry. "So maybe we should all get some dog training."

Jessie looked at Watch, who wagged his

tail. Watch belonged to all four of the Alden children, but he was a bit more Jessie's dog than anybody else's. Jessie thought Watch was perfect the way he was. But maybe a refresher course would make him even more perfect—if that was possible. "Okay," she admitted. "Maybe Watch could use a tiny reminder."

Watch jumped up and down and barked.

* * * *

Later that afternoon the four children rode their bikes to Dog Gone Good. Watch came with them, of course.

The outside of Dog Gone Good was newly painted in bright red. The parking lot had space for a dozen cars.

"This is a very yellow bike rack," said Benny as they parked their bikes.

"And it's shaped like a dog," said Henry as he inspected the wire rack. "Do you know what kind?" he asked his brother.

"It looks like one of those long low dogs," answered Benny.

"Those are called dachshunds," said a voice from behind them.

Benny and Henry turned to see a tall man wearing white pants, a white shirt, and a white apron. "Hello," he said. "I'm Baker Brooks." Mr. Brooks had a dog with him, and Watch rubbed noses with it.

The Aldens introduced themselves.

Violet and Benny were looking at Mr. Brooks's dog. It was a big white dog with black spots all over. "It's a Dalmatian," Violet said to Benny.

"Like the dogs that ride on fire trucks," said Benny.

The Dalmatian wagged its tail. Violet noticed that the dog's eyes were a pale blue, almost violet in color. Just then, the Dalmatian sat down and put out a paw to shake hands with her.

"Boxcar likes you," Mr. Brooks told her. "He doesn't shake paws with just anybody."

Violet put out her hand and shook the dog's paw.

"Your dog is named Boxcar?" asked Henry.

He was thinking about the boxcar he and his sisters and brother had lived in.

"Yes," said Mr. Brooks.

"Did you find him in a boxcar?" asked Benny.

"No," said Mr. Brooks. "I love trains. I go out of my way to see them. And I especially love boxcars, so that's how I named my dog." He reached down and patted Boxcar's head.

"Are you taking Boxcar to class?" asked Jessica.

"Yes, I am," said Mr. Brooks. "Boxcar needs to learn the *stay* command."

"We're taking Watch to class, too," said Jessie. "May I ask you a question about your name?" she asked Mr. Brooks.

Mr. Brooks laughed. "I'll bet I know what it is. I'll bet you want to know if Baker is my first name or my title."

"I hope it's not rude to ask," said Jessie.

"Not at all," said Mr. Brooks with a smile. "Almost everybody asks me that sooner or later."

The children waited eagerly to hear the answer. Mr. Brooks seemed to enjoy keeping them in suspense. "Well," he said at last, "Baker is my first name. But I always say that my mama knew I would be a baker when I grew up, and that's why she named me Baker."

Mr. Brooks reached into his white apron and pulled out a small loaf of bread—it was shaped like a bone. "This is one of the special dog breads I bake," he told the Aldens. "Dogs love it." He handed the bread to Benny.

Benny couldn't help himself, he put the bread to his nose and sniffed it. "Yum," said Benny. "It smells so good!" Benny loved food.

"It *is* good," chuckled Mr. Brooks. "But it's for your dog, Benny, not for you."

The other Aldens watched to see if Benny would give up the bone-shaped bread. Watch jumped up and down, then sat and begged for the bread. Finally, Benny fed it to Watch.

"Don't worry," said Mr. Brooks to Benny. "I have something for you, too."

"Bread?" asked Benny.

Mr. Brooks pulled some papers out of another pocket. He counted out four, and handed one to each of the children. "This is a coupon for a free coffee, tea, or lemonade when you buy bread at my bakery," he said. "Please visit soon."

"We will," said the Aldens. Although they teased Benny, they had all loved the smell of Mr. Brooks's bread.

"Come on, Boxcar," said Mr. Brooks. "Time for class." He and Boxcar walked into the Dog Gone Good building.

Benny was staring at his coupon. "Can we go right after Watch's class?" he asked. "I'd really like some bread."

"We can't go today because we promised to help Mrs. McGregor," Jessie reminded him. Mrs. McGregor was the Aldens' housekeeper and cook. "But we'll go as soon as we can," she promised.

As the children and Watch walked toward Dog Gone Good, a white van pulled into the parking lot. The words *Clip and Yip* were painted on its side in black letters. Below the words was the outline of a French poodle. Below the outline were smaller words: *Dog Grooming Deluxe*.

Jessie and Watch walked into the building first. Benny, Violet, and Henry followed.

"Hello!" said Roxanne when she saw them. "I'm so glad you and Watch are coming to this class."

"We're glad, too," said Henry.

The room was full of dogs and people. Jessie noticed that Mr. Brooks was handing out bread bones to the dogs and coupons to the people.

Henry noticed that one woman didn't seem to have a dog. She had come in just after the Aldens. She had curly light brown hair and wore a white apron that had many pockets. Henry wondered if maybe she was a baker, too. Just as he was wondering, the woman came up to them.

She looked at Watch. "That's a wire-haired terrier," she said. "Which of you is the owner?"

"Watch is Jessie's dog," explained Henry,

"but we all think of him as our dog."

"Your dog could use some grooming," the woman said. She stuck out a coupon and waved it around.

Jessie thought the woman was a little rude. Jessie reached out to take the coupon. "I'm Jessie Alden," she said. Then she introduced her brothers and sister.

"I'm Candy Wilson," said the woman.

Benny's eyes grew bigger. "Do you own a candy store?" he asked.

Candy Wilson frowned. "I own Clip and Yip, the best dog grooming service in six towns." Then she bent down to look at Watch.

Jessie didn't like how Ms. Wilson inspected Watch, looking at him from every side as if she had to memorize him for a test. Ms. Wilson petted Watch. He seemed to enjoy it.

Ms. Wilson stood up. "Bring your dog to my store and I'll improve his looks," she said. "Plus, you get twenty percent off with that coupon."

Then she turned away and walked up to another person and waved a coupon.

When it was time for the class to begin, Roxanne introduced all the owners and their dogs.

"We have six dogs in this class," she said. "And we have eight owners." She introduced Mr. Brooks and Boxcar, and after that she introduced Henry, Jessie, Violet, and Benny. And Watch, of course.

"That dog has four owners!" a man pointed out.

His name was Victor Smith, and his bulldog was named Wrinkles.

Benny thought that was a good name for a bulldog. "Wrinkles has a lot of wrinkles!" he said to Jessie.

Roxanne introduced the next dog owner, who had two little dogs that looked exactly alike. One dog wore a red collar and leash, the other wore a blue collar and leash. Both dogs were barking. "Everybody say hello to Mrs. Garrett and her twin Pekinese, Double and Trouble," said Roxanne.

The Aldens and everybody else said hello, but Mrs. Garrett was too busy to say hello back. She was trying to untangle herself from the red and blue leashes as Double and Trouble raced around and around her.

Roxanne frowned. "By the end of this class, Double and Trouble will not be doing that," she promised.

Jessie thought Roxanne didn't sound too sure about her promise.

Roxanne continued. "Our last dog owner is Mrs. Servus," she said. "She owns a a beautiful malamute named Grayson."

"Grayson *Majesty*," corrected Mrs. Servus, who was standing next to the Aldens. Her dog sat beside her. It was a big dog, mostly gray and white. It looked a bit like a wolf.

"What a beautiful dog," said Violet.

Mrs. Servus overheard her. "Yes," she said, "Grayson Majesty is beautiful."

"He has such blue eyes," said Violet.

"He does *not!*" said Mrs. Servus. She jerked on the dog's leash and the two of them walked away, to the other end of the room.

Violet was embarrassed. "Did I say something wrong?" she asked Jessie.

Jessie shook her head. "No," she answered. "I don't know why Mrs. Servus got upset."

Roxanne clapped her hands. "Okay, owners! Okay, dogs! Time for class to begin!"

Everyone lined up in rows with their dogs, except for Candy Wilson, who didn't have a dog. She waved to the class. "Goodbye, everybody!" she shouted. "I have grooming appointments all day today and tomorrow, but I can always make room for your dogs. Be sure to visit Clip and Yip!"

Ms. Wilson reached into the pocket of her apron and pulled out two shiny tools. She waved them over her head in a circle, then left. Henry thought one of the tools must be a clipper, and the other a pair of special scissors.

For the next half hour Roxanne taught some basic commands, such as *sit* and *come*. Then she worked with each dog and each owner, one at a time.

As class came to an end, Roxanne taught the *stay* command. Each owner told his dog to stay. Henry said "stay" to Watch, and Watch sat still. Henry looked over at Mr. Brooks and Boxcar. The Dalmatian seemed to be staying put.

Nearly all the dogs seemed to obey, except for Double and Trouble, who kept yipping and running in circles. Roxanne went up to each Pekinese and pushed its rear end down to the floor. "Stay!" she commanded. The two Pekinese sat down and stopped yapping.

"Roxanne is very good," Jessie said softly.

Henry nodded. He thought Roxanne was doing a great job with so many different dogs and owners.

"Now," said Roxanne to the dog owners. "I want each of you to tie your dog's leash to a post. After you do that, we will all quietly leave this room. We'll walk into the next room and close the door. We'll stay there for five minutes. And when we come out, our dogs should still be sitting and waiting for us."

"What?" said Mr. Smith. "I don't think Wrinkles is ready to be left alone yet."

"Five minutes is a long time," said

Mr. Brooks as he looked at Boxcar. "Can we make it two minutes instead?"

Roxanne shook her head. "Don't worry," she said. "Your dogs are better than you think they are." She frowned at the Pekinese as she said this.

Everybody did as they were told. The dogs stayed put as the owners walked away.

In the next room Roxanne closed the door. She talked to everyone about why it was important to have a well-trained dog. "A well-trained dog is a happy dog," she said. "It will feel comfortable around you and around people you meet."

"Can we go out now?" asked Mr. Smith.

"Just a minute," said Roxanne. "I need to check on something."

She walked out of the room.

A few moments later, Roxanne was back. She looked at her watch and said, "Five minutes are up."

When the owners stepped out into the training room, the door to the outside was open. There was an empty space where

Boxcar had been sitting.

Everybody stopped and stared at the empty space.

"Where's Boxcar?" asked Benny.

CHAPTER 2

Searching for Boxcar

Mr. Brooks ran outside and began shouting for his dog. "Boxcar! Boxcar! Where are you?"

Roxanne looked very worried. "Oh, no," she kept saying. "Oh, no."

Jessie patted Watch on the head. "Good dog," she said.

"Poor Mr. Brooks," said Violet. "It looks like Boxcar really won't stay."

"Did Boxcar run away?" Benny asked.

"It looks that way," said Jessie.

Henry looked at the place where Boxcar had been tied. Henry didn't understand how Boxcar could have gotten himself and his leash off the post. But maybe he could—dogs were smart.

The other owners were petting their dogs and praising them for staying. Even Double and Trouble had done well.

"We should help Mr. Brooks look for Boxcar," said Violet.

The other Aldens agreed. The children and Watch went outdoors. Mr. Brooks was walking up and down the parking lot, calling out his dog's name. The children helped him look. They checked in the nearby park and on three side streets, but there was no sign of the Dalmatian dog anywhere.

When the children returned to the parking lot, Roxanne led everybody back into the Dog Gone Good building. She explained to the class that Boxcar had run away. "I have to teach another dog training class," she said. "But if you have time to help Mr. Brooks, please do."

"We have time," said the Aldens.

Mr. Smith and Mrs. Servus also helped search, but there was no sign of Boxcar. After a while Mr. Brooks said he would go back to his bakery to see if Boxcar went there.

The children looked for another hour, but Boxcar seemed to have vanished.

As they walked to the Bread Loaf Bakery Benny asked, "Do you think Boxcar went back to the bakery?"

"I hope so," said Violet. "I hate to think of a dog lost and all alone."

"If I were a dog, I'd go home to the bakery every day," said Benny.

But when the children entered the bakery, they could tell by the look on Mr. Brooks's face that his dog had not returned.

"Thank you for helping," said Mr. Brooks. He gave them a loaf of bread. "Oh, no," said Jessie, "you don't have to do that. We're always glad to help."

"Please take it," said Mr. Brooks. "I want to show my thanks."

Jessie took the bread and thanked him for it.

"We can keep on helping you," said Henry. "If you have a picture of Boxcar, I can scan it into our computer. Then I can make flyers with Boxcar's picture."

"Really?" asked Mr. Brooks. "You'd do that?"

"Yes," said Jessie. "We love to help. Tomorrow morning we can come back, and if Boxcar isn't home yet, we can take flyers into all the stores around here."

Mr. Brooks gave Henry a picture of Boxcar. Jessie pulled out her notebook and asked him to describe Boxcar. She wrote down a description. Then she wrote Mr. Brooks's phone numbers.

"You are making me feel better," Mr. Brooks said as they were leaving. "You are making me feel as if we'll find Boxcar."

"We are good at finding things," said Henry. "We'll find Boxcar for you."

During dinner that night the children told Grandfather and Mrs. McGregor all about the dog training class. They also told about how Boxcar was missing at the end of the class, and how they were going to help Mr. Brooks by making flyers.

"That is a kind thing to do," said Grandfather. "Do you still want to go to Northport with me tomorrow?" he asked, "Or will you spend the whole morning helping Mr. Brooks?"

"If we went to Northport, would we have time to visit the computer store?" asked Henry. The children's favorite computer store was in Northport.

"Yes," said Grandfather.

The children talked it over and decided they could help Mr. Brooks and still be back in time to go to Northport with Grandfather.

"Let's make that flyer for Mr. Brooks right now," said Jessie.

The children helped clear the table, then went to Henry and Benny's room.

Henry scanned the photo of Boxcar into the computer.

Violet wrote a headline: *Lost Dalmatian Dog*. "We could print the headline in purple," she said.

Jessie typed a description of Boxcar. She also wrote information on when and where Boxcar was last seen, and who to call if he was found.

Henry printed fifty leaflets and Benny put them in a large envelope for the next morning.

"These are excellent flyers," said Mr. Brooks the next morning.

"Thanks," said Henry. "Our plan is to go into stores for four blocks in every direction and ask if we could put them up."

Jessie and Benny went in one direction, and Henry and Violet went in another.

Jessie was very happy that almost every store owner agreed to put a flyer in the store window.

Benny carried the flyers. "Look," he said, pointing to a large sign that hung from a store roof. "That sign is shaped like a French poodle."

"Yes," said Jessie. "So that must be Clip and Yip." But when Jessie tried the door, it was locked. "Oh," she said, "that's too bad.

Ms. Wilson might have been able to give us ideas about where a lost dog would go."

Jessie looked around for a list of the store hours, but there wasn't one in the window or on the door. *That's strange*, she thought. She knew that most stores posted their business hours.

Benny and Jessie continued going to stores and asking them to post flyers about Boxcar. By ten o'clock they were done. So were Henry and Violet.

The Aldens rode their bikes home, and then Grandfather drove them all to Northport.

He parked the van in front of the dentist's office. "I'll be done by noon," said Grandfather. "We can meet at the diner."

Grandfather went into the dentist's office. The children set off for the computer store.

"Look," said Benny as they waited at a street corner. "There goes Ms. Wilson in her van."

The others looked up in time to see the Clip and Yip van turn left.

"Her store wasn't open this morning," said Jessie. "We couldn't post a flyer there."

"I wonder what she's doing in Northport," said Violet.

"Maybe she makes house calls," said Jessie. "You know, somebody who has a dog that needs to be groomed calls Clip and Yip, and Ms. Wilson comes to the house."

"Maybe," said Henry, "but most people take their dogs to the groomer's."

"Let's go see if we can find her van," said Benny. "We could give her a flyer to post in her store."

The children crossed the street, then they turned left on the same street the van had gone down. They didn't see it the street. But when they looked around, they saw the Clip and Yip van at last. It was parked in an alley.

The Aldens stood there, wondering where Candy Wilson could be. Jessie looked at the stores around them.

"*Dogs*," said Benny. "What's that other word?" He was pointing at the corner store. Benny was just learning to read.

The other children looked at the store. "You can sound out the first three letters," said Henry. "You've seen them before."

"*Yip,*" said Benny, reading. "The store is called *Dogs—Yip* something. I'll get it," he said. Benny tried again and read: "*Dogs—Yippee!*"

"That's very good!" said Jessie.

"A lot of people must like the word *yip,*" said Benny. "There's Clip and Yip and there's Dogs—Yippee!"

Henry chuckled. "Maybe," he said. "Or maybe just one person likes the word. Let's go in and find out."

The children looked into the store window, which was full of dog things. There were dog beds, dog biscuits, leashes, collars, dog toys of all kinds. They walked into the store. Candy Wilson was standing behind the counter writing something. She looked up. When she saw the Aldens, she frowned.

"What are you four doing here?" she asked. "I thought you lived in Greenfield."

Jessie thought Ms. Wilson was not friendly. Jessie explained about Grandfather and the dentist. "This is a very nice

store," said Jessie, looking around. "Do you work here?"

"Did you come to buy something for Watch?" asked Ms. Wilson.

Jessie noticed that Ms. Wilson had not answered her question.

The Aldens explained why they were there, and they gave Ms. Wilson a flyer with Boxcar's picture on it. "Will you put this up in your Greenfield store?" asked Henry.

Ms. Wilson took the flyer and read it. "Yes," she said, "I'll put this up in my Greenfield store. It's very sad when a dog is lost."

Violet thought it was very nice of Ms. Wilson to help. Maybe she wasn't so unfriendly after all.

Barking sounds came from the back of the store. "I hear dogs," said Benny.

"I sell puppies and dogs," said Ms. Wilson. "But I'm busy now."

Jessie felt like Ms. Wilson wanted them to leave. "We'll go now," she said. "Thank you for taking the flyer about Boxcar."

"Lost dogs are hard to find," said Ms.

Wilson. "I'll do all I can to help."

As the children were walking out the door, she called after them. "Don't forget to bring your dog to Clip and Yip for a grooming."

After visiting the computer store, the Aldens met Grandfather for lunch. They told him about Candy Wilson. "She must own two businesses, one in Greenfield and one in Northport," said Grandfather. "That's not uncommon."

"They're both dog businesses," said Benny as he finished his chicken pieces.

"That's good business sense," said Grandfather. "That way, some customers might buy at both places."

"Yesterday Ms. Wilson gave us a twenty-percent-off coupon if we go have Watch groomed," said Jessie.

"Does Watch need grooming?" asked Grandfather.

"Yes," said Henry and Violet together.

"Maybe," said Jessie at the same time.

"No! I don't want Watch to look like a French poodle!" Benny joined in.

Grandfather and the children all laughed together. "Well," said Grandfather. "We have a difference of opinion here."

"Watch is looking a bit scruffy," said Violet.

Jessie frowned. "Maybe just a tiny bit," she admitted.

"But don't worry," said Henry to Benny. "Whatever we decide, we won't let Watch look like a French poodle."

The children rode their bikes to the second dog training class at Dog Gone Good. Watch ran alongside them.

Today there was a new dog and new owner in the class. The dog was reddish colored, with a droopy jaw and loose skin. The man had black hair cut very, very short. He stood straight and seemed to be studying all the windows and doors.

"Wow!" said Benny. "That dog has even more wrinkles than Wrinkles!"

"I heard that," said the man as he walked up to them. "My name is Mike Kovack. My dog is named Christie. She's a bloodhound."

Mr. Kovack shook hands with each of the

children as they told him who they were. Then he looked at Watch. "Nice dog," he said. He squatted down and looked at Watch very closely.

Just then Roxanne walked into the large room. She wore a bright yellow shirt.

Benny stared at her.

Mr. Kovack noticed Benny. "What are you looking at?" he asked Benny.

"Roxanne's hair," answered Benny. "I love how red it is."

"It's dyed," said Mr. Kovack.

"How do you know?" asked Benny.

"Look at the roots," said Mr. Kovack. "You can always tell the true color by looking at the hair roots. Roxanne's roots are dark brown."

"Oh," said Benny. Then he added, "I still like it."

Mr. Kovack was about to say something, but just then Mr. Brooks walked in the door. All the other dog owners asked if Boxcar had been found. Mr. Brooks shook his head.

"I'm so sorry your dog ran away," said Roxanne.

"Boxcar did not run away," said Mr. Brooks in a loud voice. "My dog was stolen—right from your dog school."

"No," shouted Roxanne. "That's not true!"

"Watch out!" Mr. Brooks warned. "Dogs have been stolen wherever Roxanne Sager works." He looked at all the owners. "Your dog might be next." Then he turned and walked out the door.

CHAPTER 3

Watch Is Groomed

At dinner that night, the children talked about what Mr. Brooks had said. Had Boxcar run away, or had he been stolen? At breakfast the next morning, they were still talking about it.

"Boxcar would not run away from all that good bread," said Benny, eating a second piece of toast.

"What did Mr. Brooks mean about Roxanne?" asked Violet. "Mr. Brooks said that dogs have been stolen wherever Roxanne worked."

Jessie started to help Mrs. McGregor clear the dishes. "Where else did she work?" asked Jessie.

Grandfather smiled as he got up from the table. "I have a feeling this is all a mystery," he said. "And I have an even stronger feeling that you four will solve it."

Henry helped clear the rest of the dishes. "Let's go talk to Mr. Brooks," he said.

"Then to Roxanne," said Violet. "We have to be fair."

"Wait," said Jessie. She put her hands in her front pockets, then in her back pockets. "Ah, here it is." She showed them the coupon for twenty percent off at Clip and Yip. "Let's do it," she said. "Let's get Watch groomed while we're in town."

Instead of taking their bikes, the children walked to town. They kept Watch on a leash. When they reached the Bread Loaf Bakery, Jessie didn't want to tie him up outside the store. "I just don't feel right leaving him alone," she said. "Especially if somebody might be stealing dogs." So Jessie stayed outside with Watch, and Henry, Violet, and Benny went into the bakery.

Nobody was behind the counter. A small silver bell stood next to a sign that said, *Ring for Service*. Henry rang the bell. The children waited, but nobody came.

"I hear voices," said Benny.

The children listened. They heard two male voices. One of the men talking was Mr. Brooks. "Selling stolen dogs is easy money," he said.

"That's true," said the other voice.

"I could get almost a thousand dollars for Boxcar," said Mr. Brooks.

The children looked at each other. They knew it wasn't polite to listen to other people's conversations in secret.

"I think there's a patio outside," said Henry. "Let's go see if Mr. Brooks is there."

The three Aldens walked toward the back of the store and out an open door. A red brick wall enclosed a small eating area. A tree grew in the middle of the patio.

"Oh," whispered Violet. "How beautiful."

Mr. Brooks sat at a far table with Mr. Kovack. The two men did not see or hear the three children.

"I would steal the malamute next," said Mr. Kovack. "Grayson."

"Hello!" said Henry in a loud voice. He noticed that both Mr. Brooks and Mr. Kovack half-jumped out of their chairs.

Mr. Brooks spoke first. "Hello," he said. "We didn't hear you come in."

"We rang the bell," said Benny.

Mr. Kovack stood up. "I must be going. I just came in to get my free coffee for buying a loaf of bread."

Henry saw that the table Mr. Brooks and Mr. Kovack were sitting at had papers and pens on it. But there was no bread or coffee.

Mr. Kovack stopped in front of the Aldens. "I know all about you," he said. "You're the children who have solved some mysteries. But you were just lucky," he told them.

"We don't solve mysteries by luck," said Henry.

Mr. Kovack looked at them. "Do you think

you solve them because you're smart?" he asked.

"Yes," said Jessie. "We think about things and we use logic to solve mysteries."

"We'll see," said Mr. Kovack. Then he left.

"I didn't know you knew Mr. Kovack," Henry said to Mr. Brooks.

"I didn't know him," answered Mr. Brooks. "He came in and somehow we started talking about dogs."

Benny wanted to say: You were talking about *stealing* dogs! But he kept quiet and listened.

Mr. Brooks asked where Jessie was. When they told him, he went outside and invited her and Watch into the patio. "Nice dog," he said, patting Watch on the head. "Terriers are very popular dogs."

"Mr. Brooks," asked Henry, "why did you say that dogs have been stolen wherever Roxanne Sager works?"

"Because it's true," Mr. Brooks answered. "Did you know that she used to work at a dog training school in Elmford? And did you know that in three months, three dogs were lost or stolen from that school?"

"We didn't know that," said Henry, "but that doesn't mean Roxanne stole the dogs."

"And after that, she worked for two months in Northport," said Mr. Brooks. "And one dog was stolen from that school."

"How do you know all of this?" Jessie asked him.

"I just know," said Mr. Brooks. "If you don't believe me, you can find out for yourselves. Now I have some bread to take out of the ovens."

Mr. Brooks went into the back of his store. The Aldens could see him. He was using a long wooden paddle to take loaves of bread out of brick ovens. The Aldens looked at one another. "I guess Mr. Brooks won't say any more," said Henry.

"Maybe we should buy some bread and get our free lemonades," said Benny. "Then Mr. Brooks might talk to us some more."

His brother and sisters laughed. "Nice try, Benny," said Henry. "But the bread and lemonade will have to wait."

"But we'll use our other coupon now," said Jessie. "The one for getting Watch groomed."

The children left Bread Loaf Bakery and walked down the street to Clip and Yip. The store was open, and Candy Wilson was grooming a dog and talking to its owner.

The Aldens saw that the dog was the gray and white malamute, Grayson Majesty. Mrs. Servus watched as Ms. Wilson used a hair dryer on Grayson.

Henry noticed that the hair dryer slid back and forth on an overhead rail. Candy Wilson finished drying Grayson and hooked the dryer to the rail over her head. Mrs. Servus walked all around her dog, looking at him from head to toe. "Hmmm," she said. "Grayson Majesty looks good. I may decide to come here once a month."

Ms. Wilson unhooked Grayson's leash from the overhead rail, then fed him a one-bite dog biscuit. When he finished eating it, she lowered the grooming table almost to the ground. "Come on, boy," she said to Grayson, and he jumped off the low table.

"I hope you do bring Grayson in once a month," she said to Mrs. Servus. "Your dog deserves the best grooming."

Then the two women noticed the Aldens. The children said hello to everyone. Grayson and Watch touched noses, but Mrs. Servus pulled Grayson away. She walked to the counter to pay her bill.

While they waited, the Aldens looked all around Clip and Yip. Henry had already noticed the electric clipper and dryers hooked to the overhead rail. Now he noticed the steel washing tubs. Henry liked everything he saw. He thought Ms. Wilson could do a very good job with all her tools.

Jessie walked around the shop. She saw the flyer about Boxcar being lost. It was posted on a bulletin board, where everybody could see it.

Violet and Benny looked at all the fun things for dogs. Benny looked at rubber balls and things that Watch could fetch. Violet looked at bandannas. She thought Watch would look good with a lavender colored bandanna around his neck.

After Mrs. Servus left, Jessie said they had brought Watch in for a grooming.

"Wonderful," said Candy Wilson. She bent down to pet Watch. She fed him a one-bite dog biscuit. Then she led him into one of the big steel tubs. The children watched as Watch got a bath. Ms. Wilson talked to Watch the whole time. Jessie thought that Watch was very calm—more calm than when he got a bath at home.

After the bath, Ms. Wilson gave Watch another one-bite treat, then led him to the grooming table and raised it. She hooked Watch's collar to a metal arm that kept him from moving around too much. "Good dog," she said as she petted him.

She looked at the children. "Now," she said. "How would you like Watch to look?"

"Just like himself," answered Jessie.

"Only neater," added Henry.

"That's easy," said Ms. Wilson. "Terriers look neat to begin with. Are you sure you want Watch to look just like he does? I could change his looks a lot."

"We like Watch the way he is," said Violet.

"Okay," said Ms. Wilson as she began to trim Watch's fur with electric clippers. "Watch isn't a show dog, is he?" she asked.

The children said he wasn't.

"He looks like a healthy dog," said Ms. Wilson as she worked. "And friendly, too," she said. "Those are the best kinds of dogs, don't you think?"

The Aldens agreed.

After Ms. Wilson finished trimming Watch's fur, she took a pair of small clippers from her apron pocket. Then she carefully clipped Watch's toenals. "There," she said after she finished. She gave Watch a last treat, then lowered the table. "Watch looks great," she said. "I'll bet he's never looked better."

Henry, Violet, and Benny agreed. Even Jessie agreed. They paid for the grooming, using their twenty-percent-off coupon for a discount. "Be sure to come back again," Candy Wilson said as they left.

"Watch looks really good!" said Benny once they were out on the sidewalk.

Watch pranced with his head high.

"Yes," admitted Jessie. "Ms Wilson did a really good job. And she was so good with Watch."

"Dogs trust her," said Violet. "She keeps them calm and happy."

"That's because she gives them doggie treats," said Benny. The others laughed.

CHAPTER 4

Dog Gone Again

After such a busy morning, the children were glad to be back home. "You all look like you need a good lunch," said Mrs. McGregor as Henry, Jessie, and Violet sat down to eat.

"Oh, my!" Mrs. McGregor said as she noticed Watch. "Whatever happened to Watch? He looks beautiful."

"Watch was groomed today," said Jessie. "Do you really like how he looks?"

"Oh, yes," said Mrs. McGregor. "He

almost looks like a different dog." She looked around. "Where is Benny? It's not like him to be late for food."

Just then Benny came running in. "I'm not late, am I?" he asked, out of breath.

"What were you doing?" asked Jessie.

"I was looking all around our boxcar," Benny answered. "Just in case Boxcar might be there."

"What makes you think Boxcar would come here?" Jessie asked.

"Well, we lived in a boxcar when we ran away," said Benny. "I thought Boxcar might do the same thing."

"Thank you for checking," said Jessie with a smile.

Mrs. McGregor put lunch on the table. The children passed around the tacos and toppings.

"I really hope Boxcar comes home soon," said Violet. "He must be sad. Maybe he's scared."

"But if Boxcar was stolen, he can't come home," said Henry.

All through lunch, the children discussed whether Boxcar was lost or stolen. They even talked about it as they rode their bikes to dog training class. Watch ran alongside the bikes.

They parked their bikes in the bright yellow bike rack. Watch ran up to the door of Dog Gone Good and barked.

"I think Watch likes going to school," said Benny.

Henry opened the door and they all entered Dog Gone Good. They almost walked into Christie, Mr. Kovack's bloodhound. She was sitting by the door.

Mr. Kovack was bending down alongside Grayson. Henry looked around, but Mrs. Servus wasn't in the room. *That's strange*, he thought.

"Hi, Mr. Kovack," said Benny, walking up to him. "What are you doing with Grayson's collar?"

Mr. Kovack was holding Grayson's leather collar. Then something fell out of Mr. Kovack's hand and rolled around on the floor. "You dropped something," said Benny.

"I'll get it." Benny stooped down to pick up the shiny silver, but Mr. Kovack blocked his way.

"I've got it," said Mr. Kovack. "Just a dime," he said, putting it into his pocket.

Benny didn't know what the silver thing was, but he knew it wasn't a dime. He wondered why Mr. Kovack had told a lie.

By this time Jessie, Violet, and Henry were all standing around Mr. Kovack and Grayson.

"You took Grayson's collar off," said Jessie. Mr. Kovack scowled at Jessie. He put Grayson's collar back on.

Violet looked closely at the big, friendly malamute dog. It *did* have blue eyes, just like she thought.

Mr. Kovack stood up. "It's a nice collar," he said. "I just wanted to see what kind it was."

The door opened again, and Mrs. Servus walked in carrying coffee and rolls. Henry went to help her.

"Here you are," she said, handing Mr. Kovack a glazed roll and a cup of coffee.

"Your roll and your free coffee from Bread Loaf Bakery."

"Thanks," said Mr. Kovack.

Henry wondered why Mr. Kovack didn't get his coffee himself. *Did he want to be alone with Grayson Majesty?* he thought.

Just then Roxanne walked into the room from her office, and Mrs. Garrett walked in the front door with Double and Trouble. The twin dogs started barking. Watch barked back at them. The two big dogs, Grayson and Christie, just looked down at the tiny dogs. Mr. Smith walked in the door with his bulldog, Wrinkles, and the dog training class began.

Roxanne began with *sit.* The owners all said "sit" to their dogs. The Aldens had agreed that only one of them at a time would talk to Watch. Benny started. When he said "sit," Watch sat. "Good dog," said Benny, patting Watch on the head.

Jessie watched the other dogs. Mr. Kovack's dog was wonderful. Christie just sat and looked around and waited. Wrinkles did well, and so did Grayson. Double sat, but Trouble would not. Finally Roxanne helped out and got Trouble to sit.

The next command was *down*. It was Violet's turn to give the command. Watch sat, but he did not lie down. Violet gently pushed him down, but he sat right back up.

Roxanne came over with some treats in her hand. "Down," she said to Watch, pushing him down gently. Watch lay down, but sat up for the treat. Roxanne wouldn't give it to him. Instead, she handed the treat to Violet. "Down," said Violet. Watch lay down. Only then did Violet give him the treat. "Good dog," she said, patting him.

"Good work, Violet," said Roxanne.

Violet smiled shyly.

Jessie was still watching the other dogs and owners. The instant that Mr. Kovack said anything, his dog did it. Jessie thought that Christie didn't need dog training. *Why is Mr. Kovack here?* she wondered.

Just then the door opened, and Candy Wilson walked in. "Hello," she called out.

"I just dropped by to see how everybody is doing. Did anybody notice how beautiful Grayson and Watch look?" she asked.

"Yes," said Mrs. Garrett as she held on to Double and Trouble. "I noticed. And I would like you to groom Double and Trouble, if you wouldn't mind coming out to my house to do it."

Ms. Wilson frowned at the two little dogs. "I'm sorry," she said, "I don't do house calls. I'll be happy to groom both dogs at Clip and Yip. Just drop in any time." Ms. Wilson knelt down to help untangle Double and Trouble's leashes.

Another door opened, and Mr. Brooks stepped out of Roxanne's office. "It's all ready," he said to her in a friendly way. "I'll just go back to my shop."

"Thank you so much!" Roxanne called after him as he left.

Violet found it strange that Mr. Brooks was being so friendly with Roxanne. *Just this morning he thought that Roxanne stole his dog!* she thought. Violet also wondered what Mr.

Brooks meant when he said, "It's all ready."

The next command that Roxanne taught was heel. She asked Mr. Kovack to give Christie the *heel* command. He did, and then he and his dog walked all around the large room. Christie heeled perfectly.

Jessie commanded Watch to heel. She thought Watch looked very good as he walked alongside her. "Good dog," she said.

When the class was almost over, Roxanne took the owners and dogs outside the building. "Now," said Roxanne as the whole group stood there. "Each of you must take your dog to a different side of the building. Tell your dog to stay. Then walk back here to meet me in the parking lot. This will be like real life, when an owner ties his dog up and goes into a store."

"I don't think Wrinkles will stay for ten minutes," complained Mr. Smith.

"Wrinkles is a good dog," said Roxanne. "He will stay."

Mr. Kovack spoke up. "I'm sorry," he said, "but neither my dog nor I can stay."

Henry thought that was quite funny.

"I have to leave early for a meeting," Mr. Kovack told Roxanne. "Come!" he called, and his bloodhound trotted after him.

"It's time for me to leave, too," said Candy Wilson. "I have more grooming appointments. Bye, everybody!" She headed toward her white van.

Roxanne clapped her hands to get everybody's attention. "Okay, owners. Take your dog to a spot near the building. Tell your dog *stay*, then come back here."

Jessie gently tugged Watch's leash and he followed her. She took Watch to the far side of the building and tied him up so that he was across from a little window.

"This is a good spot," she told Watch. She commanded him to stay, and then she walked back to the parking lot.

When all the owners except Mr. Kovack were back in the parking lot, Roxanne told them she had a surprise. "I always give treats to good dogs," she said. "Now I have treats for all you good owners."

"Oh, boy," said Benny.

"Let's all go to my office for lemonade and cookies," said Roxanne. "Mr. Brooks made them, so you know they are delicious. After ten minutes, we'll all go outside and see how your dogs are doing."

The dog owners followed Roxanne toward her office. Just before they reached the door, Jessie whispered, "Wait!" to her brothers and sister. After all the owners were inside Roxanne's office, Jessie pointed to a door down the hallway.

"That's the women's washroom," she whispered. "I'm going to stay in there and look out the window to make sure nobody steals Watch."

"Good idea," said Henry.

Jessie went into the washroom. She stood on a radiator and peeked out the window at Watch. Jessie was proud that Watch was still sitting and waiting for her.

Then she saw Mr. Brooks walk by. *What's he doing here?* thought Jessie. He was supposed to be going back to his shop. As she

watched, Mr. Brooks stopped to pat Watch on the head. Then he kept walking.

Next, Jessie heard the sound of a car motor. It seemed to be going very fast. But she couldn't see the car itself.

Violet came into the washroom. "Is Watch okay?" she asked her sister.

"So far," said Jessie.

"Roxanne left the room for a few minutes," said Violet. "But she came back. Now she says it's time to go see our dogs," said Violet.

Jessie and Violet joined the others. They walked out of the Dog Gone Good building. Together, the owners walked out of the building and around it. Double and Trouble were in the first spot. They were not sitting. Their leashes were all tangled up. "Oh, dear," said Mrs. Garrett as she started to untangle everything.

Around the corner was Wrinkles, who was sitting. "Good dog," said Mr. Smith, giving Wrinkles a treat.

Watch was around the other corner. He was still sitting. "Good dog," said Jessie, as she gave Watch his treat.

"Two bad dogs and two good dogs," joked Mrs. Servus as they turned the last corner. "Grayson Majesty will of course be a good—" suddenly Mrs. Servus screamed. "Grayson! Grayson! Where is he? My dog is gone!"

CHAPTER 5

Blue Eyes

Roxanne looked at Grayson's leash, which was still tied to a small tree. "Your dog broke his leash and ran away," she said.

Suddenly Mr. Kovack and his bloodhound came running from the nearby park. "What's wrong?" asked Mr. Kovack. "I heard somebody scream."

"Grayson Majesty is gone," cried Mrs. Servus. "Please help me find him. He broke loose from his leash."

"We'll help you find him," Violet said to Mrs. Servus.

"Yes," said Jessie. "Maybe we should start looking right now?" she asked Roxanne.

But Roxanne wasn't listening. She was looking at Mr. Kovack. "I trusted you," she said. "Now look what's happened."

Henry wondered what Roxanne meant about trusting Mr. Kovack. He also wondered what Mr. Kovack was doing here. "You said you couldn't stay," Henry said to him. "But you're still here."

"I took Christie for a walk first," answered Mr. Kovack.

Henry picked up the end of the leash that wasn't tied to the tree. There was no ragged tear across the leather. Instead, there was a very clean cut. "This leash wasn't broken," said Henry. "It looks like somebody cut it."

"Let me see that," demanded Mr. Kovack. He looked at the leash, then he looked at Henry. Roxanne looked over his shoulder. "This leash has been cut," said Mr. Kovack. He turned to Mrs. Servus.

"I'm sorry," he said, "but it looks as if somebody cut this leash and took your dog."

Mr. Kovack rolled up the leash and put it in his pocket.

"Took?" asked Mrs. Servus. "You mean stole? Grayson has been *stolen?*" Mrs. Servus was very upset. She was pacing around in circles, waving her arms.

Violet felt very sorry for her.

All at once Mrs. Servus stopped in front of Roxanne. "This is your fault," she shouted. "You run a training school where dogs are stolen!"

"N-n-no, I don't," said Roxanne. "I don't know why this is happening."

Now Violet felt bad for Roxanne.

"You are in big trouble," Mrs. Servus told Roxanne. "Grayson Majesty is a purebred malamute. He's worth big money! He's a valuable show dog."

"That's not true," said Mr. Kovack.

Everybody turned to look at him.

"What's not true?" asked Jessie.

"It's not true that Grayson is a valuable show dog," Mr. Kovack said.

"Yes, he is!" said Mrs. Servus. She turned

to Roxanne. "He's worth big money and I'm going to make you pay."

"No," begged Roxanne. "Please don't do that."

"We'll help you find your dog," Henry said to Mrs. Servus. "We're good at finding things."

But nobody listened to what Henry was saying. Everybody was shouting at everybody else.

"Your dog isn't a valuable show dog because he isn't a purebred malamute," said Mr. Kovack to Mrs. Servus.

Mrs. Servus gasped. "Yes he is. My dog is a purebred malamute!"

Mr. Kovack just shook his head. "No," he said. "Your dog has blue eyes. Only dark-eyed malamutes are purebred. The ones with blue eyes can't enter shows for purebred malamutes."

Now Mrs. Servus was even more upset. She was so upset she began to hiccup and couldn't speak.

Violet remembered what Mrs. Servus had

said about her dog's eyes the first day of class.

"Mrs. Servus must want people to think that Grayson is a show dog," she whispered to Jessie. "That's why she wouldn't admit he has blue eyes."

"Please don't be upset," Henry told Mrs. Servus. "It doesn't matter what color your dog's eyes are. He's still the best dog in the world to you."

Mrs. Servus looked at Henry gratefully. She nodded her head. "Yes. I just want him back." Tears filled her eyes.

"I think we should start looking for Grayson," Jessie said.

"Yes," said Henry. "Right now."

"You kids are right," muttered Mr. Kovack. "Henry, can you take charge and lead the search?"

"Sure," said Henry.

Mr. Kovack turned to Roxanne. "I'd better get to my meeting," he said. "But you can help with the search."

"Uh, well, uh," said Roxanne. "I mean, I can't help search. I'd like to, but I have to get ready for my next class. Sorry about that."

Violet noticed that Mrs. Servus frowned at Roxanne.

Henry organized everybody into four groups. He sent each group in a different direction, with instructions to ask questions to everyone they met.

Roxanne stayed behind. So did Mr. Kovack, who hadn't left yet.

"I'll watch your dogs for you," Roxanne told the dog owners.

But nobody wanted to leave their dogs with Roxanne. Everybody took their dog with them.

Jessie and Mr. Smith were on the same team. Watch and Wrinkles seemed to like each other.

Jessie and Mr. Smith walked by the Bread Loaf Bakery. They asked Mr. Brooks if he had seen Grayson Majesty.

"You mean he's missing?" asked Mr. Brooks.

"I'm afraid so," answered Mr. Smith. "His leash was cut. We're afraid he was stolen.

And Roxanne won't help us look."

Mr. Brooks was silent. Finally, he spoke. "I don't think Roxanne stole Boxcar or Grayson," he said.

"What made you change your mind?" asked Jessie.

"Roxanne is just too good a person to steal a dog," Mr. Brooks replied. "She came to my shop at lunch and we had a long talk. She told me she would never steal a dog. I believe her. That's why I made cookies and lemonade for the class."

After the Bread Loaf Bakery, Jessie and Mr. Smith visited five more stores and talked to six people on the street. Then they reached Clip and Yip.

Mr. Smith tried to open the door, but the store was closed. "Why isn't Clip and Yip open?" he asked. "How can I bring Wrinkles here if the store isn't open?"

"I don't know why it's not open," said Jessie. "It was open yesterday, when we took Watch in for grooming."

At the end of an hour, all the searchers met

in the Dog Gone Good parking lot. They checked inside the building to see if Grayson had returned. He hadn't.

Mrs. Servus was very sad. "Please don't worry," said Jessie. "We will help you find your dog." She told Mrs. Servus that she and Henry and Violet and Benny could make a poster of Grayson and put it in store windows.

Mrs. Servus gave them a picture of Grayson Majesty and Jessie wrote down all the information about him.

"You can say that he has blue eyes," said Mrs. Servus. "That might help somebody recognize him."

"Okay," said Jessie.

As the children walked out to their bikes, Mr. Kovack came from behind the building.

Mr. Kovack looked at the Aldens. "You kids probably wonder why I'm still here."

"Yes," said Henry. "You said you had a meeting."

"I'm still here because a stolen dog is more important than a meeting," said Mr. Kovack. Then he walked away.

Lost Dog

"Maybe he never had a meeting," said Henry. The others nodded. It was hard to tell when Mr. Kovack was telling the truth.

When the Aldens got home they put their bikes away and fed Watch. Then they made another Lost Dog flyer. They printed out fifty copies.

Benny took a flyer and looked at it. "I wish we knew who stole Boxcar and Grayson," he said.

Violet looked at the flyer, too. She noticed something. "Boxcar and Grayson both have blue eyes!" she said.

"That's true," said Henry.

"Do you think it means something?" asked Jessie.

But no one had the answer to that.

CHAPTER 6

Notebook Time

"You are all very quiet," said Grandfather at dinner.

"Yes," said Mrs. McGregor. "I've never heard you all so quiet."

"Henry," said Grandfather, "tell me what you're thinking about."

"Scissors, clippers, and knives," answered Henry as he buttered a slice of bread.

Grandfather looked at Henry. "Please explain why," he said.

"They can all cut through a leather leash,"

answered Henry. “I want to know if each cut looks different.” Henry cut a piece of steak and looked at the knife cut. “Maybe Watch has an old leash that I can experiment on,” he said.

“I have an old leather belt,” said Grandfather. “You can use that.”

“Thanks!” said Henry.

“And what about you?” Grandfather asked Jessie. “You aren’t thinking about scissors, clippers, and knives, are you?”

Jessie shook her head. “I’m thinking about whom dogs will go with.”

Violet asked Jessie what she meant.

“Well,” explained Jessie, “take Watch. If Roxanne asked him to do something, he would. If Mr. Brooks gave him a bread bone, Watch would follow Mr. Brooks. And if Ms. Wilson gave him a doggie treat, he would go with her.”

“I like Mr. Brooks,” said Benny. “He makes good bread.”

“Yes, he does,” said Mrs. McGregor as she cleared the plates.

"I'm thinking about something, too," Violet said to Grandfather. "I'm thinking about dogs with blue eyes."

"What do you mean? Grandfather asked.

"Both the missing dogs had blue eyes," Violet explained.

Benny looked around as Mrs. McGregor walked into the room. "Is that apple crisp for dessert?" he asked.

"Yes, it is," she said.

"Yum," said Benny. "I'm thinking about food."

"I am not surprised," said Grandfather. He chuckled.

"But I'm thinking about dogs and food," said Benny. "I'm thinking about what food a dog likes best."

"If you were a dog," teased Jessie, "what food would you like best?"

"I'd like Mr. Brooks's bread bones the best!" Benny said. "I like them the best, and I'm not even a dog!"

That evening, the children met in Jessie and Violet's room.

"It's notebook time," said Jessie, pulling out a notebook and pen. "Let's make a list of what we know about the person who might have stolen the two dogs."

"Let's start with Roxanne," said Henry, "because we met her first."

"Roxanne is very good with dogs," said Benny. "She can get Watch to do anything."

Violet spoke. "Do you remember that Roxanne was gone from the room each time a dog was missing?" she asked.

Henry and Jessie nodded.

"Why would Roxanne steal dogs?" asked Benny.

"She could make money by selling the dogs," explained Henry.

Jessie shook her head. "That's true, but if dogs are stolen from Dog Gone Good, that hurts Roxanne's business."

The others nodded.

Jessie wrote on one page of her notebook:

Roxanne

—can get dogs to follow her

—was missing when dogs were stolen

"The next person we met was Mr. Brooks," said Benny. "He gave us a bread bone for Watch."

"That's right," said Henry. "What can we say about Mr. Brooks?"

"He can get a dog to follow him by giving it a bread bone," said Benny.

"Yes," said Henry. "And we heard him say that selling stolen dogs is easy money."

"But Mr. Brooks would never steal his own dog, would he?" asked Violet. "He couldn't do that to Boxcar."

"There's something you don't know," said Jessie. "When I was in the washroom keeping an eye on Watch, I saw Mr Brooks walk by and talk to Watch. But Mr. Brooks was supposed to be gone already, remember?"

"I remember," said Violet. "He brought rolls and lemonade for everybody, then he left to go back to work."

"Mr. Brooks accused Roxanne of running a class where dogs were stolen," said Henry. "But the next day, he and Roxanne were friends again. Maybe the two of them are a team that steals dogs."

Jessie turned to a new page of her notebook and wrote:

Baker Brooks
—can get dogs to follow him
—said that selling stolen dogs is easy money
—was around Dog Gone Good when Grayson was stolen
—accused Roxanne of stealing Boxcar, then changed his mind

"The third person we met was Ms. Wilson," said Violet. "She was giving out coupons to all the owners."

"Ms. Wilson can get dogs to follow her," said Benny. "She gives them doggie treats."

"Yes," said Henry, "and she keeps cutting tools in her apron. Look," he said, pulling out the old belt Grandfather had given him. "I made this cut with a knife," he said, pointing to one end of the belt. "And I made this second cut with a pair of scissors."

"What do you think?" asked Benny.

"I think that Grayson's leash was cut with a pair of scissors," said Henry. "I just don't know what kind of scissors."

"Or whose scissors," Violet pointed out.

Jessie clicked her pen a few times. "Ms. Wilson seems very interested in every dog," she said. "She asks questions about it. And she was visiting Dog Gone Good when each dog was stolen."

"Ms. Wilson goes everywhere in her van," added Benny. "To her store in Greenfield and to her store in Northport." Benny bounced up and down on his chair.

"And, Ms. Wilson likes the word *Yip!*" Benny added.

The others laughed. "That's true, Benny," said Jessie. "Is that good or bad?"

"Good," said Benny.

Jessie used a third page of her notebook and wrote:

Candy Wilson
—can get dogs to follow her
—has sharp cutting tools
—asks a lot of questions about each dog
—owns a store that sells puppies and dogs

"There is only one person left to think about," said Violet.

Jessie nodded. "Mike Kovack."

"There are a lot of suspicious things about Mr. Kovack," said Henry. "He told Mr. Brooks that the malamute would be stolen next. That's Grayson. And Grayson *was* stolen next!"

"Mr. Kovack is very good with dogs," said Violet. "Dogs just seem to listen to him and do what he says. And," she said, "Mr. Kovack was doing something to Grayson's collar."

"Yes," said Jessie. "Whatever it was, he didn't want us to know about it."

Violet looked puzzled.

"What are you thinking?" Henry asked her.

"About Christie, Mr. Kovack's dog. She's the best trained dog I've ever seen," answered Violet.

Henry nodded. "That's right. So I wonder what Mr. Kovack is doing in dog training school. Maybe he's there to steal dogs."

"There's a problem with that," said Jessie.

"Mr. Kovack wasn't there Monday afternoon, when Boxcar was stolen."

Henry thought about this for a while. "That's true," he said. "But today Mr. Kovack said he had to leave for a meeting. Then, when Grayson was stolen, Mr. Kovack came running. And he stayed the whole time we were searching. I think Mr. Kovack lied about having a meeting." Henry scratched his head and thought a bit longer. "And Roxanne seemed very upset with Mr. Kovack. I wonder if she thinks he stole Grayson Majesty."

"Mr. Kovack lied about the dime," said Benny.

"What dime?" asked Henry.

"The shiny thing that fell from Grayson's collar," said Benny. "Only I saw it, and it wasn't a dime. Mr. Kovack put it in his pocket."

Henry snapped his fingers. "That reminds me! After I said that Grayson's leash had been cut, Mr. Kovack took the leash and put it in his pocket!"

"Mr. Kovack is very suspicious," said

Jessie as she turned to another page of her notebook. She wrote:

Mike Kovack
—dogs obey what he says
—seemed to know which dog would be stolen next
—tried to do something to Grayson's collar, then Grayson was stolen
—lied about the shiny thing that fell from his hand
—lied about needing to go to a meeting when Grayson was stolen
—took Grayson's leash after Henry said the leash had been cut

After she had finished writing, Jessie read the notes out loud.

"Wow," said Benny. "Somebody is stealing dogs, but I don't know who."

That night before the children went to sleep, they agreed they had to talk to some people the next day.

CHAPTER 7

Watch's Collar

"We gave out all our flyers about Grayson Majesty," said Violet as she and Henry met up with Jessie, Benny, and Watch. The children had biked to town after breakfast. They had divided into two teams and visited stores.

"We did, too," said Jessie.

"I sure hope Mrs. Servus gets her dog back soon," said Violet "And Mr. Brooks, too."

"Now we'll get right to work on the mystery," said Henry.

Benny led the way to the Bread Loaf Bakery.

There was a new handwritten sign on the door. It said, *Dogs Welcome*.

"I guess that means we can take Watch inside," said Jessie.

"Hello, Mr. Brooks," said Benny as the children entered the shop. "Have you found Boxcar yet?"

"No," said Mr. Brooks.

"We've come to buy some rolls and get our free lemonades," said Benny. He clutched the coupon in his hand and almost pressed his nose to the glass case. Jessie pulled him back just in time, before he smeared the sparkling clean glass.

The Aldens each picked a roll, and they also bought a bread bone for Watch. Mr. Brooks told them they could sit on the patio. When he brought their lemonades, Jessie asked if they could ask him a few questions.

"Sure," he said. He pulled up a chair from another table and sat down next to Watch. "Watch looks great," said Mr. Brooks. "I almost wouldn't recognize him."

"You told us that Roxanne worked at other dog training schools where dogs were stolen," said Henry. "How did you learn that?"

Mr. Brooks looked uncomfortable. "I feel bad that I accused Roxanne," he said. "I apologized to her. I was just upset about my dog, that's all."

Henry asked his question another way. "You said that when Roxanne worked in Elmford and Northport, there were dogs stolen," said Henry. "How did you know that?"

"I read it in the newspaper," answered Mr. Brooks. "Here, let me show you." He reached over to a shelf and pulled a newspaper off it. "See," he said, spreading open the paper to the personal ads. A few of them were circled in red ink.

Jessie and Violet looked closely at the small ads. "These ads are from owners still looking for their lost dogs," said Jessie.

"And the dogs went missing from dog training centers," said Violet.

"So," said Henry, "dogs might have run away from nearby dog training centers. Or, they might have been stolen."

"Stolen," said Mr. Brooks. "Somebody is stealing dogs from training centers. Maybe one or two dogs a month. Maybe more."

"That's bad," said Jessie.

"That's terrible," said Violet.

Henry looked at Mr. Brooks. "But how did you know that Roxanne worked at these two places?" asked Henry.

"I called the two places and talked to the owners. I asked who was working there when the dogs went missing. Roxanne worked at both places."

"Hmmmm," said Henry. "That doesn't look good."

"But like I told you before, Roxanne came over to talk to me," said Mr. Brooks. "I'm convinced she didn't steal any of the dogs. Roxanne and I are friends again."

This made Violet feel very good. She liked Roxanne, and she liked Mr. Brooks.

"If you don't suspect Roxanne anymore,

whom do you suspect?" asked Jessie.

Mr. Brooks looked away.

The children waited.

"Well," said Mr. Brooks at last, "Mr. Kovack seems to know a lot about stolen dogs."

"We overheard you and Mr. Kovack talking," said Henry. "It sounded to us like you were both talking about stealing dogs."

Mr. Brooks jumped out of his chair. "I forgot! There's bread in the oven! Sorry, I have to tend to business, can't answer your questions right now." He left the patio.

The Aldens watched Mr. Brooks rush away.

"That's strange," said Benny, finishing his glazed roll. "Mr. Brooks always runs to his ovens whenever we ask him questions."

"Maybe his bread needs a lot of attention," said Jessie. "Or maybe Mr. Brooks just doesn't want to answer certain questions."

The children finished their food. When they paid for it, there were four other customers in the shop. Mr. Brooks really was busy.

"Let's go talk to Roxanne next," said Benny. "I like her red hair, even though it has brown somethings."

"Roots," Violet explained to her younger brother. "Each hair on your head grows out of a hair root in your scalp."

Benny felt his head. "My hair is brown," he said. "So my hair roots must be brown, too."

"That's right," said Henry. "If you dyed your hair red, your roots would still be brown. That's why people who dye their hair have to dye it again every few weeks."

"Mr. Kovack knew that Roxanne dyes her hair because he noticed her brown hair roots," said Jessie. "Mr. Kovack notices a lot of little things like that," she said.

"Look," said Henry as they walked into the Dog Gone Good parking lot. "That's Mr. Kovack's car."

When the Aldens walked into the building, Mr. Kovack and his bloodhound were there. Mr. Kovack was standing all alone, writing something in a notebook. Christie was sitting by his side, waiting.

Watch barked and ran up to Christie.

"Hi, Mr. Kovack," said the Aldens.

He turned around. "What are you doing here?" he asked as he put away his notebook.

"We came to talk to Roxanne," said Benny.

Watch ran circles around Christie. The bloodhound just sat there.

"Watch! *Sit!*" said Henry. "*Sit.*"

Watch stopped running, but he did not sit.

Mr. Kovack stood in front of Watch. Mr. Kovack lifted a finger and pointed it at Watch. "Sit," he commanded.

Watch sat next to Christie.

"You're very good with dogs," said Violet. "They do whatever you want."

"I like dogs," said Mr. Kovack. "And Watch is a good-looking dog."

"Christie is a very well-trained dog," said Henry.

Mr. Kovack started to say something, then stopped.

"We wonder why you and Christie are in a dog training class," said Jessie.

"What do you mean?" asked Mr. Kovack.

"Neither of you needs any training," said Jessie.

Mr. Kovack chuckled. "Everybody needs a refresher course."

Just then the door to Roxanne's office opened, and Roxanne stepped out. "Oh, hi everybody," she said. "This is way too early for class."

"The Alden kids want to talk to you," Mr. Kovack told her.

Roxanne turned pale. "Oh," she said. She looked around nervously. "Well, maybe you should all come into my office."

The children stepped forward. "Come, Watch," said Jessie.

Watch stood up to follow her.

"Wait," said Mr. Kovack. "Why don't you leave Watch with me while you talk to Roxanne? I'll spend the time going over the basic commands with Watch."

"Oh, no, that's okay," said Jessie. "We'll take Watch with us."

"You're worried that something will

happen to Watch," said Mr. Kovack. "But nothing will happen to him. I would never hurt Watch. He's safe with me."

Jessie still hesitated.

"Look," said Mr. Kovack, "I will stay right in this room and I won't let Watch out of my sight."

Jessie looked at Watch, who wagged his tail.

"Watch and Christie can be together," said Mr. Kovack.

Roxanne spoke up. "Mr. Kovack will take very good care of Watch," she said. "I know he will."

"Well," said Jessie. "Okay." She looked at Watch. "Stay!" she ordered. And then the children walked into Roxanne's office.

Benny was the last one in. He made sure he did not close the door all the way. He left it open just a little, so he could look over his shoulder into the training room. Benny heard Mr. Kovack telling Watch and Christie *down!* Both dogs lay down.

"I know why you're here," said Roxanne,

sitting at her desk. She put her head down and held it in both hands. "You want to take Watch out of training class, and you want your money back."

"Why would we do that?" asked Jessie.

Roxanne looked sad. "Because you're afraid your dog will be stolen," she answered.

"We don't want to take Watch out of your class," said Jessie.

"It's a good class," added Violet. "We like coming to it."

Roxanne looked up. "Really? Then why are you here?"

Benny looked over his shoulder again. Mr. Kovack was walking in big circles all over the room, and Christie and Watch were following him, one on each side.

"Is it true that you worked at two other dog training places?" asked Henry. "One in Northport and one in Elmford?"

With a moan, Roxanne put her head back in her hands. "I know what you're going to say," she said. "Dogs ran away from both of those places. You wonder if I had anything to do with it, don't you?"

"Maybe they ran away," said Henry, "or maybe they were stolen."

Roxanne moaned again. "I didn't steal them," she said. "I don't know who did, but—" Roxanne stopped.

Violet, Jessie, and Henry all looked at her. "But, what?" asked Jessie.

"I shouldn't tell you this," said Roxanne, "but I'm doing something about it."

The children looked at each other. "What are you doing?" asked Violet.

Roxanne shook her head. "I can't tell you." Benny looked over his shoulder. Mr. Kovack was kneeling in front of Watch. He had taken Watch's collar off and was holding it in his hands!

CHAPTER 8

A Cover Uncovered

Benny tugged on Jessie's arm. "Look," he whispered.

Jessie turned to see what Benny was doing. She noticed the door that he had left ajar. "Good work, Benny," she whispered back.

Jessie looked through the open crack. She saw Mr. Kovack holding Watch's collar in his hand. Then she saw Mr. Kovack put the collar back on Watch.

"Excuse me," Jessie said to everybody. "We need to see Mr. Kovack and Watch. Right away."

Henry and Violet turned to see what was the matter. They followed Jessie and Benny out the door. "Excuse us," said Henry to Roxanne.

Mr. Kovack was just standing up as the children approached him.

"Watch," Jessie called. "Come!"

Watch ran to Jessie. "Sit!" she said, and Watch sat.

"See how much better your dog listens," said Mr. Kovack.

"Why did you take off Watch's collar?" Benny asked.

"Who, me?" asked Mr. Kovack.

"I saw you," said Benny.

Mr. Kovack grunted. "You kids see everything, don't you?"

The Aldens said nothing. They waited.

"Watch's collar was loose," said Mr. Kovack. "I took it off then put it back on, that's all."

Roxanne came out of the office. "What's going on?" she asked. "Is there a problem?"

"We'll see," said Henry. He looked as Jessie

knelt down and took Watch's collar off.

Jessie looked at the outside of the collar. She looked at the inside of the collar. She looked at the buckle. Jessie didn't see anything strange. She was confused.

"See," said Mr. Kovack. "There's nothing wrong."

"Let me see," said Henry. Jessie gave him the collar, and he examined it closely. At first it looked fine, but then Henry noticed a very thin line on the inside of the collar. It looked as if somebody had cut the leather. Henry ran his thumbnail alongside the line. Yes, it was a cut. He pushed his thumbnail into the cut to open the slit up. Henry felt something inside the slit. He took it out and held it in his hand. It was a small, very thin piece of metal, like a dime, only thinner.

"What's that?" asked Violet.

"I'm not sure," said Henry, "but I can make a good guess." He looked at Mr. Kovack. "I think this is a small tracking device."

Mr. Kovack looked away.

"Let me see," said Benny. He looked at the

small silver disc. "This looks just like what fell out of Mr. Kovack's hand when he took Grayson's collar off. Mr. Kovack said it was a dime, but it isn't."

Roxanne looked down at the floor.

"Why did you put this in Watch's collar?" asked Henry. "Were you planning to steal him?"

Mr. Kovack sighed. Then suddenly he smiled, and then he laughed. "You kids really are good detectives," he said.

He looked at Roxanne. "I guess I have to confess," he said.

"I guess so," she said.

Mr. Kovack reached into a pocket and pulled out his wallet. He opened the wallet and pulled out a card. He handed the card to Henry.

The card said:

Mike Kovack
Private Detective
No Case Too Small

Henry handed the card to Jessie, who read it out loud.

"Are you really a private detective?" Jessie asked.

"Yes," said Mr. Kovack.

"How do we know this card is for real?" asked Henry. "Anybody could have a business card printed up."

"That's true," Mr. Kovack replied. "But I have an office in Silver City, and I'm listed in the phone book."

"He really is a private detective," said Roxanne. "I hired him Monday night, after Boxcar was stolen."

"That's why Mr. Kovack's first day of dog training class was Tuesday," said Violet.

"And that's what you're doing about the stolen dogs," said Jessie to Roxanne. "You hired a private detective."

Roxanne nodded.

"I was trying to put one of those tracking devices on Grayson Majesty," Mr. Kovack explained. "But Benny saw me, and I had to stop."

"We overheard you and Mr. Brooks," said Henry. "You said that the malamute would be the next dog stolen."

"And I was right," said Mr. Kovack.

"Do you suspect Mr. Brooks?" asked Violet. She hoped not.

"I can't share that information with you," said Mr. Kovack.

Jessie wasn't thinking about Mr. Brooks. She was thinking about what Mr. Kovack had said—about trying to put the tracking device on Grayson. "Mr. Kovack," she said, "do you think that whoever the thief is, he might try to steal Watch next?"

At the sound of his name, Watch looked up and barked happily.

"You're right," Mr. Kovack answered. "I think that if another dog is stolen from this class, it will be Watch."

Jessie knelt down and put her arm around Watch's neck. "Why?" she asked.

Mr. Kovack looked at Watch and smiled. "Watch is a wire-haired terrier. He's a very good-looking dog. He's a happy dog. He's fun to be with. That makes him easy for a thief to sell."

The Aldens agreed with Mr. Kovack's description of their dog. Benny, Violet, and Henry formed a circle around Watch to protect him.

"We can't let that happen!" cried Violet. "Watch is our dog. He wouldn't be happy without us."

"We *won't* let it happen," said Henry firmly.

Mr. Kovack looked sympathetic. "You told me that Watch doesn't have papers that show his breeding. You don't enroll Watch in dog shows. And that," he said, "also makes it easy for a thief to sell Watch."

"How do you mean?" asked Jessie, still kneeling and holding Watch.

"I mean, if Watch had papers and could be traced, if Watch was recognized by people who go to dog shows, the thief would have a harder time not getting caught. Somebody might recognize Watch and report it to the police."

"I see," said Henry. "The thief wants a dog that will sell for a lot of money, but the thief doesn't want the dogs that would sell for the *most* money."

"Because the dogs that sell for the most money are better known," said Violet.

"The thief is very sneaky," said Benny. "Maybe he would make the dogs look different."

"That's true," said Mr. Kovack. "But he couldn't make them into show dogs. Anyway, we're going to find out who the thief is, aren't we?"

"Yes," said the Aldens together.

"Good," said Mr. Kovack. "Do you think we should keep the tracking device in Watch's collar?"

"Yes," said Jessie.

Everybody watched as Henry put the little disc into the slit in Watch's collar. Jessie fastened the collar back onto Watch.

"I am very impressed with what you kids have learned so far," said Mr. Kovack. "Who do you suspect the thief is?"

"I'm sorry," said Henry, "but we can't share that information with you. Not until we're sure."

Mr. Kovack laughed. "Spoken like a true detective," he said.

CHAPTER 9

More Blue-Eyed Dogs

After dog training class was over, the Alden children stood in the parking lot of Dog Gone Good.

"Let's talk to Ms. Wilson," said Jessie. "We haven't had a chance to ask her about the missing dogs."

"Good idea," said Henry.

The children looked for Candy Wilson, but they couldn't find her or her van. Clip and Yip was closed.

Jessie peeked into the window of the

closed store, but she couldn't see anybody there. "Something about this bothers me," said Jessie.

"What bothers you?" asked Benny.

"Do you remember what Ms. Wilson said the first day of class, as she was leaving?" asked Jessie.

"She said she had to leave because she had grooming appointments," said Henry.

"That's right," said Jessie. "But what did Benny and I find when we searched for Boxcar that day?"

"Clip and Yip was *closed!*" said Benny.

Jessie smiled at Benny. "That's right. And what did Ms. Wilson say two days later, as she was leaving class?" Jessie asked. "Just before Roxanne asked us to tie our dogs up outside the building."

"Ms. Wilson said the same thing again," said Henry. "She said she had grooming appointments. That could only mean appointments at Clip and Yip," he explained. "She doesn't make house calls."

"And there are no dog grooming tools at

her Northport store," added Violet.

"Not long after Ms. Wilson left, Grayson Majesty was stolen," said Jessie slowly. "Mr. Smith and I walked by Clip and Yip, to ask her if she had seen Grayson. But her store was closed."

"Ms. Wilson told a lie," said Benny.

"We need to talk to Ms. Wilson," said Henry.

After breakfast the next morning, the children walked into town again. Clip and Yip was still closed.

That afternoon, the Aldens waited in the Dog Gone Good parking lot, hoping to see Candy Wilson's van. But once again, Ms. Wilson didn't come to class.

"There's no reason she should be here," said Violet. "She's given a coupon to everybody in the class."

The Aldens waited in the parking lot so long that Roxanne came out to get them. "Time for class," said Roxanne.

"We're sorry," said Jessie. "We were waiting for Ms. Wilson."

Roxanne bent down to pet Watch. "Candy Wilson usually comes to the first two or three classes, to give out coupons. Then she doesn't come again until I teach a new group."

"Did she come to the places you used to work?" asked Henry.

"Yes," said Roxanne, still bending down to pet Watch. "Ms. Wilson has come to every class I've taught. She says the classes bring her a lot of business."

Benny stepped closer to Roxanne. He stared at her hair.

Roxanne stood up and led everybody to class.

"I saw Roxanne's hair roots," Benny whispered to Violet. "They're brown, just like Mr. Kovack said."

"That's what happens when hair is dyed," said Violet. "Pretty soon the real color grows in again."

Before dinner that evening, Henry called Clip and Yip and left a message. He said who he was and asked if the four of them could come in the next morning or afternoon.

"Please call back," he said, and left their home telephone number.

Nobody called back that evening. Nobody called back the next morning.

The children looked at one another. "I know where we can probably find Ms. Wilson," said Jessie.

"Yes," said Violet. "Grandfather has another dental appointment Tuesday morning."

On Tuesday the children piled into Grandfather's van.

"You all seem very eager to get to Northport," said Grandfather as he drove. "Do you want to buy something at the computer store?"

"No," said Benny. "We need to talk to Ms. Wilson."

"Why?" asked Grandfather.

"I'm sorry," said Benny, "but we can't share that information with you. Not until we're sure."

Grandfather burst out laughing. So did Henry and Jessie and Violet.

"Why, Benny," said Grandfather, "you

sound like a very serious detective."

"Mr. Kovack thinks I am," said Benny. "He thinks we're all good detectives." The children had told Grandfather all about Mr. Kovack.

Grandfather parked the car near the dentist's office. "Come back to the dentist's office if you're done early," he said. "If you aren't done early, we will meet at our usual restaurant at noon."

The children walked down the side street to Dogs—Yippee!

"It's open!" shouted Benny, seeing the *Open* sign in the window.

Once again, the Aldens walked into Dogs—Yippee! Once again, Candy Wilson was behind the counter. She was writing something on a sheet of paper. Once again, she did not seem happy to see them there.

"What are you doing here again?" she demanded.

"We'd like to talk to you," Jessie said.

"We left a message at your other store," said Henry, "but you didn't call back."

"Your dog doesn't need another grooming so soon," snapped Candy Wilson. "That's why I didn't call back. And I don't have time to talk to you—I'm busy."

The children looked at one another. They had talked about what might happen if she wouldn't answer their questions.

"In that case," said Henry, "we'd like to see the dogs and puppies you have for sale."

Ms. Wilson stopped writing. She put down her pencil. "No," she said.

The children had talked about this, too.

"Are you afraid to let us see your dogs?" asked Jessie. "Do you have something to hide?"

Candy Wilson scowled at them. Then she moved from behind the counter. "I have nothing to hide," she said. "The dogs are in back."

The Aldens followed her. They waited while she unlocked the door leading to the puppies and dogs.

The children stepped into a very clean kennel room. Henry noticed that there were

about twenty dogs. Jessie noticed that the cages were large and clean.

"These dogs are very well-groomed," said Violet.

"Of course," said Ms. Wilson. "I groomed each one myself."

"You said you could make a dog look different," said Jessie. "Could you make it look so different that nobody would recognize it?"

"I don't know what you're talking about," snapped Ms. Wilson "Why don't you take a quick look at the dogs and then leave."

Benny stopped in front of each cage and looked at each dog. None of the dogs looked like Boxcar or Grayson.

Jessie stopped in front of a large white dog. It looked sort of like a Dalmatian. The dog barked happily. It tried to lick Jessie's face.

Violet knelt in front of the cage and looked into the dog's eyes. They were blue! Almost a violet-blue. As Violet looked, the dog sat down and put out its paw for a handshake. Violet shook the dog's paw.

"This dog has blue eyes," said Violet, "just

like Boxcar."

"This dog isn't Boxcar," said Ms. Wilson.

"It shook my hand, just like Boxcar," said Violet.

"This dog isn't Boxcar," repeated Ms. Wilson. "Look at it—it doesn't look like Boxcar, does it?"

"What kind of dog is this?" asked Henry.

"It's a Dalmatian," said Candy Wilson. "Its spots haven't come in yet, but they will." She paced back and forth. "Leave that dog alone," she said. "You can't have it, it's already sold."

Henry knelt down and patted the all-white dog. Henry ran his hands up the dog's fur. Near the dog's skin, he noticed that some of the hairs had black roots.

"This dog's fur is white," said Henry, "but some of the roots are black."

"That's—that's right," answered Ms. Wilson. "That's where its black spots will come in. I think you should come back another time," she said. "Like next week. I'll have better dogs next week."

"Look," said Violet. She was looking at

an all-black dog. "Is that a malamute?" she asked.

"Uh, yes," said Ms. Wilson. "But that dog has been sold, too, so just leave it alone."

"It has blue eyes," said Violet.

"So?" said Ms. Wilson. "Why do you care about blue eyes?" she asked.

Henry explained that Violet liked everything violet and purple and lilac, and sometimes blue things, too. As he explained this, Henry knelt down and petted the malamute. He ran his hand up the dog's black fur, so he could see the color of the hair roots. Underneath the black fur, Henry saw light-colored roots, gray ones and white ones.

Henry stood up. "Thank you for showing us your dogs," he said to Ms. Wilson.

"I told you I had nothing to hide," she said as she led them out of the room.

Once they were outside, Henry spoke. "That black malamute is not really black," he told his sisters and brother. "Its fur has gray and white roots."

"Ms. Wilson dyed its fur!" said Jessie.

"And the white dog had white fur with black roots," said Benny. "She must have dyed its fur, too!"

"The white dog was Boxcar," said Violet. "I know it was Boxcar."

The children walked directly back to the dentist's office. They found an empty bench on the sidewalk and sat down. Henry pulled out the cell phone that Grandfather made sure they took with them.

"It's time to make some phone calls," said Henry.

CHAPTER 10

Reunion!

By the time Grandfather was done at the dentist's, Henry had made all the phone calls.

"Should we have lunch while we wait?" asked Grandfather.

Henry shook his head. "Everybody will be here soon," he said. "And I think we should act quickly."

"That's right," said Jessie. "We've been watching to make sure that Ms. Wilson's van is still there."

Just as she said that, a car pulled up and

parked. Mr. Brooks and Mrs. Servus stepped out of the car. "Here we are," said Mr. Brooks.

Another car pulled up and parked. Mr. Kovack stepped out of the car. "Everybody's here," he said. "Good work, Henry and Jessie. Good work, Violet and Benny."

Grandfather introduced himself to Mr. Brooks and Mrs. Servus and Mr. Kovack. "My grandchildren always do good work," he said with a smile.

The group of eight people walked down the side street and into Dogs—Yippee!

Candy Wilson looked very nervous. "What are you all doing here?" she demanded. "I'm about to close. You'll have to come back another time."

"I'm here to see the Dalmatian dog you have for sale," said Mr. Brooks.

"And I'm here to see the malamute you have for sale," said Mrs. Servus.

"Those dogs have already been sold," said Ms. Wilson.

"We want to see them anyway," said Mr. Brooks.

"We sure do," said Mrs. Servus.

"No," said Candy Wilson. "You wouldn't like these dogs. They aren't as nice as your dogs were."

Benny walked up to the locked door in the back of the store. "The dogs are back here," he said. Mr. Brooks and Mrs. Servus followed him.

"We won't leave until you unlock this door," said Mr. Brooks.

Candy Wilson jangled her big key ring and walked to the door. "All right, all right," she complained. "I have nothing to hide."

She unlocked the door. Benny walked into the kennel room. Mrs. Servus and Mr. Brooks followed him. Everybody else walked into the kennel room, too.

As soon as Mrs. Servus and Mr. Brooks stepped into the room, two dogs started barking. The barks were very loud and very happy.

Mr. Brooks ran up to the all-white Dalmatian, which was jumping around in its cage and barking. Mr. Brooks knelt down and the

Dalmatian licked his face.

"Boxcar!" said Mr. Brooks. "What happened to you—where are your spots?" He petted Boxcar and tried to hug him through the cage.

"That's white dye," said Henry. "Ms. Wilson dyed his spots so that he would look different. If you ruffle Boxcar's fur, you can see black roots where his spots are."

Mr. Brooks looked. "You're right," he said.

"That's ridiculous!" said Ms. Wilson.

Mrs. Servus was trying to hug the all-black malamute, which had its paws on the cage and was trying to get out.

"Grayson!" she said. "I'd recognize you anywhere! You have such beautiful blue eyes!" She also tried to hug her dog through the cage.

Mrs. Servus turned toward the Aldens. "I suppose that Grayson has been dyed black?"

"Yes," said Henry. "If you ruffle his fur, you'll see white and gray roots underneath."

"That's ridiculous," said Candy Wilson. "Utterly ridiculous."

Mrs. Servus faced Candy Wilson. "Unlock this cage at once," she demanded.

Candy Wilson stood there, unsure what to do. Mr. Kovack reached over and took the key ring from her hand. Then he found the right keys to unlock the cages that Grayson and Boxcar were in.

Both dogs jumped out and jumped up to lick their owners. Mr. Brooks and Mrs. Servus hugged their dogs.

Mr. Kovack chuckled. "Now is not the time to say down, is it?" he asked everybody.

Mr. Brooks turned to face Candy Wilson. "You stole our dogs," he said.

Candy Wilson looked very nervous. "I found these dogs," she said. "They were roaming the streets."

"No," said Henry. "You stole these dogs from the Dog Gone Good training center. You gave them dog biscuits so they would know you. Then, when we were all in the office, you took the dogs. You used a pair of your grooming scissors to cut Grayson's leash."

"You put each dog in your van," said Jessie. "And you drove away. Nobody could see the dog in your van. I heard a car drive away when Grayson was stolen. It was your van."

"I found these dogs, that's all," said Ms. Wilson.

"You changed the way they looked," said Violet. "But you couldn't change the color of their eyes."

"Such beautiful eyes," said Mrs. Servus, hugging Grayson.

"I agree," said Mr. Brooks, hugging Boxcar.

"Ridiculous," said Ms. Wilson. "Why would I steal your dogs."

"We know why," said Mr. Kovack. "Boxcar and Grayson are beautiful dogs. They are popular breeds. You could get a lot of money for each dog. But neither dog is a show dog. So you wouldn't have to worry about somebody recognizing the dog."

Mr. Kovack pulled out his cell phone. "It's time to call the police," he said.

Later, after the police had come and taken statements from everybody, Grandfather and the children left Dogs—Yippee! So did Mr. Kovack, Mrs. Servus, and Mr. Brooks. So did Grayson and Boxcar.

Candy Wilson had left in the police car. She was going to have to answer a lot of questions.

"Thank you for finding Boxcar," said Mr. Brooks to the children. "Now I'm happy again."

"Yes," said Mrs. Servus, "thank you for finding Grayson. I love my dog."

Henry, Jessie, Violet, and Benny watched as two people and two dogs piled into Mr. Brooks's car. They waved goodbye as the car drove away.

Mr. Kovack turned toward the children. "I want to thank you, too," he said. "I was working on the case, but you were the ones who solved it."

"We had to think hard to solve this mystery," said Jessie.

Mr. Kovack nodded his head. "You solved the mystery because you're smart—not because you're lucky." He gave each of them

a business card. "When it comes time for you to get a job, you should consider detective work," he said.

Grandfather smiled. "Maybe they will," he said. "But until then, I think my grandchildren still have a lot more adventures ahead of them."

Then Mr. Kovack got in his car and drove away.

Benny turned toward the corner restaurant. "I know we're smart," he said, "but sometimes we're lucky, too. Like now. It's way past lunch time, and we're standing next to a restaurant."

The Aldens all laughed as they followed Benny into the restaurant.